little Miss Trouble

by Roger Hargreaves

PSS!
PRICE STERN SLOAN

"Here comes trouble," people used to say.

And who do you think would come walking along?

That's right!

Little Miss Trouble.

Oh, the trouble she caused.

One morning she went to see Mr. Uppity.

"Do you know what Mr. Small calls you behind your back?" she asked him.

"No," replied Mr. Uppity. "What does Mr. Small call me behind my back?"

Little Miss Trouble looked at him.

"Fatty!" she said.

Now, Mr. Uppity didn't like that.

Not at all.

Not one little bit.

He went immediately to see Mr. Small.

"How dare you call me FATTY!?" he shouted.

"But . . ." stammered Mr. Small, who never had called him Fatty.

"But . . ."

"But nothing," shouted Mr. Uppity.

And he hit poor Mr. Small.

Ouch!

And gave him a black eye.

Poor Mr. Small.

Little Miss Trouble, who was hiding behind a tree, hugged herself with glee.

"Oh, I do so like making trouble," she giggled to herself.

Naughty girl!

Little Miss Trouble went to see Mr. Clever.

"Do you know what Mr. Small calls you behind your back?" she asked him.

"No," replied Mr. Clever. "Tell me! What does Mr. Small call me behind my back?"

Little Miss Trouble looked at him.

"Big Nose!" she said.

Now.

Mr. Clever didn't like that very much either.

Off he rushed.

And, when he found Mr. Small, without waiting for an explanation, he punched him!

Hard!

In the other eye!

Poor Mr. Small.

Two black eyes for something he'd never done.

"Oh look at you," Little Miss Trouble laughed when she saw him.

"It's all your fault," said Mr. Small.

"True," she said.

And walked off.

Poor Mr. Small had to go to the doctor.

"Good heavens!" exclaimed Doctor Makeyouwell when he saw him. "Whatever happened to you?"

Mr. Small explained.

"I think," Doctor Makeyouwell said when he'd heard what Mr. Small had to tell him, "that something should be done about that little lady! What she needs is . . ."

Then he stopped.

And he chuckled.

"That's it," he laughed.

"What's it?" asked Mr. Small.

And Doctor Makeyouwell whispered something to Mr. Small.

Would you like to know what he whispered?

Not telling you!

It's a secret!

That afternoon Mr. Small went to see Mr. Tickle.

"Do you know what Little Miss Trouble calls you behind your back?" he asked.

"No," said Mr. Tickle. "What does Little Miss Trouble call me behind my back?"

Mr. Small looked at him.

"Pudding Face!" he said.

Then Mr. Small went to see Mr. Bump.

"Do you know what Little Miss Trouble calls you behind your back?" he asked.

"No," said Mr. Bump. "What does Little Miss Trouble call me behind my back?"

Mr. Small looked at him.

"Mr. Nitwit!" he said.

Little Miss Trouble was in trouble.

"How dare you call me Pudding Face?!" cried Mr. Tickle.

And tickled her.

"And how dare you call me Mr. Nitwit?!" cried Mr. Bump.

And bumped her.

Now, I don't know whether you've ever been tickled and bumped at the same time, but it's not much fun.

In fact, it's no fun at all.

Ticklebumpticklebumpticklebumpticklebump!

For ten minutes.

And ten minutes of ticklebumping is a long time.

I can tell you!

Later that evening Doctor Makeyouwell strolled around to see Mr. Small.

"How are the eyes?" he asked.

"Oh much better now thank you," replied Mr. Small.

"And did our little plan work?" asked the doctor.

"It did indeed," grinned Mr. Small.

"Shake," said Doctor Makeyouwell.

And they shook hands.

Well.

Not quite hands.

Doctor Makeyouwell then strolled over to see Little Miss Trouble.

She was feeling very sorry for herself.

"What's wrong with you?" he asked her.

And she told him all about it.

All about everything.

Doctor Makeyouwell looked at her.

"Cheer up," he said. "You know what you've just had, don't you?"

Little Miss Trouble shook her head.

"A taste of your own medicine," he chuckled.

And went home.

For supper.